Benjamin S. Parker

Hoosier Bards with Sundry Wildwood

and other rhymes

Benjamin S. Parker

Hoosier Bards with Sundry Wildwood
and other rhymes

ISBN/EAN: 9783337271466

Printed in Europe, USA, Canada, Australia, Japan

Cover: Foto ©Andreas Hilbeck / pixelio.de

More available books at **www.hansebooks.com**

Yours Sincerely
Benj'S Parker

Hoosier Bards

WITH SUNDRY

Wildwood and Other Rhymes

By

BENJAMIN S. PARKER

Author of " The Cabin in the Clearing," etc.

CHICAGO

CHARLES H. KERR & COMPANY

175 DEARBORN STREET

1891

TO ALL LOVERS

OF THE BIRDS AND TREES THIS LITTLE
VOLUME IS AFFECTIONATELY

DEDICATED,

BY ONE WHO IS NOT ASHAMED OF HIS KINSHIP
WITH THE WILD LIFE OF WOOD
AND STREAM.

PRESS OF THE COURIER COMPANY, NEW CASTLE, INDIANA.

CONTENTS.

PREFACE.

If any reader has been tempted to peruse
this little volume by the promptings of curi-
osity, or a desire to see what one Indiana
rhymer could find, either good or ill, to say of
his neighbors who are poets, I trust he will
permit me to arrest him at the threshold long
enough to disabuse his mind of any such no-
tion. I have certainly not set myself up as a
critic — either wholesale or retail — of the
Hoosier poets who are striving (many of them
with merited success) to deserve the good
opinions of their fellow-men. Far be it from
me to attempt such a hazardous task. Poets
can talk back, and some of them wield trench-
ant as well as graceful pens. The bards of
whom I have written neither talk nor write,
wherefore it is reasonably safe to experiment
with their feelings. That they can sing with
an excellence exceeding praise none will gain-
say. "But why," says one, "do you name
these tuneful neighbors of ours 'Hoosier
Bards?' they are not peculiar to Indiana. No
such 'pent-up Utica restrains their powers' nor
can it claim them as wholly its own." The ob-
jection to my title, thus presented in the form
of a query, is, perhaps, well taken. I grant
that our favorite singing birds are common

to a wide area. but to me they are ''Hoosier
Bards'' because it was in the wild woods of
Indiana that I first learned to know them and
to rejoice in their singing. and wherever I
have heard them since they have always re-
newed for me the rude but happy surround-
ings of the backwoods Hoosier home. Of the
other things in the volume there is nothing
for me to say save to express the hope that
they may give pleasure and even profit to
some without being a source of regret to any.

B. S. P.

THE SMELL of pennyroyal in the woods,
  The pungent tingle of the spicewood's bark,
Gray squirrels feeding on the hickory buds
  With frisk and chatter; where the woods are dark
The call of some lone bird above her nest,
Whose sorrow haunts yet not disturbs the breast:

These call and won me from the noisy town
  When first the red-bud dons her purple shroud
And blossom-snows from hawthorns patter down,
  Where bees hum low and frogs are gladly loud,
At clearing-edge or in the thicket's heart
To note each touch of Nature's artless art.

Here with my Lowell ready at command,—
  O, freedom-loving Lowell, bard divine!
What would I not have given t'have touched thy hand
  And felt one thrill of thy great pulse in mine!
Thou who, possessed of wit's Damascan steel,
Used its keen edge but for the common weal '—

Thus, oft when spring awakes the sleeping land,
  I love to wander crooning some old tune,
Some thought the trees and birds understand,
  The haunting dream of some sweet afternoon
And from such passages I weave the sheaf
Of rhyme-entangled blossom, bird and leaf.

HOOSIER BARDS.

Within his shadowy, lone retreat,
  The brown thrush pipes a silver song;
Brief, mellow, penetrating, sweet,
  Its echoes cling and linger long
In forest aisles and by the rims
  Of dead'nings, where the rabbits hide
And bluebirds chant their vernal hymns,
  As violets waken wonder-eyed.
O, hermit poet! Shunning all
  The loud-tongued fame that others seek,
And singing but to love's low call
  Where silence dwells by swamp and creek;
No seas that beat their stormy capes,
  No mountains blue in frozen air,
Inspire thee when thy genius shapes
  To wild-wood music all things fair;
Condensing into one brief strain
  The anthemed chorus of the woods,
Springs spicy fragrance after rain,
  The laughter of the falling floods,
The subtle, vibrant soul and sense
  Of leafy solitudes, the art
Of artless things, the crisp, intense
  And awesome joy the woods impart.

High on the orchard's topmost spray
  The jay repeats his rolic call;
A harlequin in blue and gray,
  A pert aristocrat, a tall,
Becheckered egotist, a beau
  Who nods and cackles and assumes —
The purblind critic ne'er would know
  The poet in such gaudy plumes;
And yet, at times his song attains
  A starlight penetrance of tone,
Like notes that fall in silver rains
  From bugles over waters blown.

Gray squirrel barking on the tree,
  Thou rustic bard of cheerful mien,
Recalling with thy ringing glee
  The bank-full brook, the woodland green,
And waking summer from her sleep;
  The blossoms rally to thy cry,
The hills grow white with wandering sheep,
  And white clouds wander through the sky,
While to the dotard's veins return
  The sap of long-departed spring:
O, jaunty squirrel! Who shall spurn
  Thy backwoods dialect's saucy ring?

A brush-heap half o'er grown with vines,
  A tangle of last summer's grass,
Where sloping west the meadow lines
  Melt into thicket and morass:
A blur of wings that hum and whir,
  An instant drop, a silent dart

Neath grass and vines and then no stir
　　Except of one, poor trembling heart:
In vain the baffled hunter's gaze,
　　In vain his eager, peering quest!
One timid bard's retiring ways
　　Preserve untorn his downy breast.

Where pasture shrubs are thick and low
　　And blue bells ring their faint perfume,
The sweet song sparrow's numbers flow
　　To time the march of bud and bloom;
And cheerily from leafless stems
　　Of blasted trees the blue birds wake
Spring's welcome echoes, by the hems
　　Of beechen wood and willowy brake.
Pied cheewinks by the garden wall,
　　Brown wrens where currant bushes throng,
Small poets are, whose lays recall
　　The humble bard's forgotten song.

March brings the noisy blackbird's joy
　　Of gusty music, rash and free:
More reckless than the truant boy
　　Who dares fate's worst in wanton glee,
His song is art's abandon, yet
　　No note is out of place, nor caught
In any discord's tangled net
　　The threads of his marauding thought.
Wild, stormy singer, brave and true
　　And leal and loyal to thy kind,
Though owls may fret and hawks pursue,
　　Thine is the free, th' unconquered mind.

When golden pippin trees are white
  Some mellow, liquid notes are heard
That mingle in one brief delight
  The thought of man, the soul of bird.
Sing on, my redbird! Strains that speak
  A tenderer hope than words can tell:
The boor who named thee for thy beak
  Had never felt the witching spell
Of wild-bird music such as cleaves
  The crust of pride and wafts the soul
From hate that blinds and care that grieves
  To love-taught art's divinest goal.

The turtle dove whose numbers move
  In mourning patience, calm, subdued,
By meadow lawn or oaken grove,
  Keeps watch above her fledging brood;
And on the dead trees hollow bole
  The gay wood-pecker plies his bill,
And "rat tat tat" his martial roll
  Rings bravely over field and hill;
His quaint call echoes loudly now,
  And now he rides the waves of light,
A swinging dory, whose red prow
  Tilts up and down in zig-zag flight.

Broad pinions checkered gray and brown,
  A breast as white as swan wings are,
An eye that from the sky looks down
  And sights the covey fleeing far;
A graceful form that soars and swings

And floats entranced in lazy ease,
  Or in swift spirals upward springs —
    A mote in dim ethereal seas.
Who sees him swooping on his prey
  Swift as dissolving meteors speed,
But pardons for its matchless way
  The cruel outcome of his deed,
And owns the hated hawk a king
  High in the eagle's royal line,
A regal bard who scorns to sing,
    But claims his rank by right divine?

Where singing grass and clover bloom
  The happy meadow-lark inspire,
He weaves in song's enchanted loom
  The music of his heart's desire.
His cheerful notes are blithe and sweet,
  As by the mint-encumbered rill,
Wild buttercups and lilies meet,
  And cowslips all their gold distill
In warbled fragrance from his beak.
  When scythes assail the grass his breast
Is troubled, and his numbers speak
  His care for mate and brood and nest.

When first the willow catkins show,
  And water elms put on a veil
Of golden glory, and the flow
  Of maple sap in trough or pail
With merry drip and tinkle makes
  The pulses leap, the fancies throng,

Then robin comes at dawn and wakes
  And gladdens all the world with song:
High on the cherry tree he tunes
  His voice to many a winsome lay,
Or in the long, sweet afternoons
  Till sunset sings his soul away.
Best bird and wise, no idle praise
  Nor foolish blame disturbs his breast;
Content, he weaves divinest lays
  Or toils at humble love's behest.
We crown him laureate of our woods
  And welcome his returning wings,
And dream of joy's beatitudes
  Whene'er the vernal robin sings.

Swift swarms of swallows dip and skim,
  And touch the cloud and kiss the stream,
And tanagers in woodlands dim
  Flash like the wonders of a dream
On dazzled senses, and are gone,
  But leave the infinite charm and stress
Of scarlet sunset, golden dawn,
  Impressed by their own loveliness.

A glint and glow of star-beams caught
  In blossom tangles, or a slight,
Swift sense of fragrance, or the thought
  The poet knows of,—dear delight,
So near, so far, so quick to fade,
  So hard to catch, so hard to hold,—
And lo, the humming bird the shade

Of summer gladness, green and gold,
And petal winged and rainbow-kissed,
  Comes quivering, flashing, pulsing by,
A meteor born of sun and mist
  In some cloud island pure and high;
A snatch of tune, a quaint refrain,
  Too brief and sweet for tardy sound,
The dreamed-of Song's liquescent Skein
  On conscious core of sunlight wound.

When finches fleck with gray and gold
  The garden walks, or chatter low
Where pea vines cluster green, or hold
  Their legislatures by the flow
Of meadow rivulets, the wheat
  On many a hillside's Southern slope
Grows yellow, and life's pulses beat
  The forward march of ripening hope.

The cat-bird in the lilac scolds,
  But yonder in the hazel dell
His crazy-quilt of song enfolds
  His sylvan world in magic spell:
All warbled strains, all woodland runes
  Run lightly through his stolen song;
A plagiarist he, to whom all tunes
  Of all the feathered choirs belong;
A tipsy Quaker quaintly clad
  In leaden garb of chaste design;
A rolic roysterer, wildly glad,
  A madman with a voice divine;

From shreds of melody and sounds
  Of native minstrelsy he spins
In many a maze of tangled rounds
  His song of songs when love begins —
When love first prompts to win and woo,
  And build the nest that leaves may hide,
To seek the grub, the moth pursue,
  And guard his prim but songless bride.

The kildeer flits above the sands
  With sharply iterated cry,
Or on the half-sunk bowlder stands
  And peers about with curious eye,
Then bows and curtsies left and right,
  Or runs along the river's brink, —
A quick, impetuous water sprite
  Who pauses not for food or drink. —
Some strange ambition haunts his thought,
  Some stranger fear his will restrains,
And brings each sudden quest to naught,
  And multiplies his restless pains.
On some lone cape where ocean sands
  Are by inconstant waters worn,
On farthest reach of barren lands
  His wild progenitors were born;
The gloom of clouds, the storm's despair,
  The pulse of waves that cry and beat,
Pursue and haunt him everywhere,
  Inspire his wings and speed his feet;
And so he bears a restless heart
  And seems a trifler impulse-torn,

A lithe winged crank whose highest art
  Is whim half-witted and forlorn.

Low broods the crow on beating wing,
  A self-sufficient egotist,
Who counts that all who toil or sing
  Must bring his mill some precious grist
To keep him always sleek and proud;
  On highway, farm, in vocal grove,
Still caw, caw, cawing at the crowd
  Of humble bards who chant of love;
A critic coarsely vain and fierce, —
  Estranged in this from critic kind —
As Lowell sings in limpid verse —
  He always heads against the wind.

Now wide-winged herons haunt the pond,
  Or fan the air in lazy flight,
And whippoorwills in woods beyond
  With plaintive outcry fill the night;
The owl with solemn hoot replies
  And dreams himself a prophet born,
While far away in hazy skies
  The wild goose honks across the corn.

When all the forest aisles resound
  With crash and boom and distant roar,
And windy tumults shake the ground
  And trees break down with feathered store,
And many swiftly-pulsing wings
  Are spread at once in sudden fright,

Till every fleeting minute brings
   The noise of some delirious flight,
And all the air is dark with swarms
   Of pigeons in their quest for food, --
While autumn leaves in eddying storms
   Are beaten by the feathered flood, —
O! then to range the woods and know
   The thrills of this gregarious joy,
Who would not leave his dreams and go
   To be again a backwoods boy,
As wild and free as bird and breeze?
   But forests melt and pigeons fade,
And their wild rhyme of thundering seas
   Is passing fast with beechen shade.

And there are other bards; alas!
   Unheeded bards and little heard
By dull-eared men whose schemes surpass,
   In their own wisdom, song and bird
And rhyme and pathos; men who make
   A jest of poetry, or dwell
Where love for greed or passion's sake
   Is tortured in a songless hell: —
So many and so little known
   By men who dream or men who mope,
But you may hear them if you own
   A gentle will, a tender hope:
They haunt the piquant, spicy woods,
   Build low in fragrant fields, or nest
Beneath the cottage eaves; their broods
   Are hid where spangled mosses rest;

Glad warbling poets, wild-wood seers,
  Sweet improvisatores of song;
They bring us back the happy years,
  The mornings when the days were long.

These minstrel bards of fields and woods,
  The vibrant air, the emerald sod,
These winged, melodious multitudes
  Are wise interpreters of God,
And swift and true their tender art
  Goes straight to nature's central core
And warms and thrills each waiting heart
  Till men stand conquered and adore.

THE BUILDING OF THE MONUMENT.

READ AT THE CAMP FIRE AT THE LAYING OF THE CORNER STONE
OF THE SOLDIERS' MONUMENT, INDIANAPOLIS, AUGUST 22, 1889.

> *Wat's words to them whose faith an' truth*
> *On war's red techstone rang true metal,*
> *Who rentered life an' love an' youth*
> *For the gret prize o' death in battle?*
> — *James Russell Lowell.*

To die in brave, unselfish sacrifice
  For friend or kindred marks the lofty soul,
Whose love exceeds all bounds of praise or price,
  Strong to the core and grandly sound and whole,
      And dowered with life that spurns the dust and
        springs
    In fame's horizon on triumphant wings.

But when a hero dies for liberty
  No pæans of praise can reach his meanest right,
No bark that sails on fame's siderial sea
  May bear aloft in history's shadow light
    Ev'n one poor tithe of his devoted worth
    To home, to country, to th' indebted earth.

Our soldiers came from all the ranks of peace,
  Were men of peace, but men whose souls were
    great
In their great love — that knew but swift increase
  When deadly perils thronged about the State, —

Their great, strong love of freedom, union,
    right,
Firm in its purpose, loyal in its might.

No monumental pile of lettered stone,
  No flight of eloquence, no lisp of song,
Nor ocean voice of multitudes, far blown
  Across the list'ning ages as they throng,
    Can recompense one mother for her dead,
    Nor heal love's anguish o'er a soldier's bed.

But yet the lettered shaft is type and sign
  Of that imperishable pile that stands
Eternal in the thought of man,—divine
  As every work of love's immortal hands,—
    Wherein all hero deeds are wrought and blent
    To one strong hope, one purpose, one intent.

That hope, intent, is freedom: Who is free?
  Not he who sees his fellows bound in chains
And robbed and torn, and bends the supple knee
  To brute assumption, or at best remains
    A cold spectator when the outcry comes
    And all the land is palpitant with drums.

This monument we raise shall long make known
  Ev'n to the stolid gazer, with no eyes
For unseen things, that freedom loves her own
  And crowns her heroes, and that nations rise
    And prosper best which most confide in man
    And forward march with freedom in the van.

O, Indiana, mother of brave men!
  Men who have hoped and dared and died for thee:
Who have enacted, for thy sake, again
    The dread obedience of Thermopylæ,
        The sacrificial strife of Bunker Hill,
        Matured in purpose, masterless in will.

Thy mother, thought, in building to their fame,
  Has bloomed in honor, may it fruit in deed
Of larger import than hope dares to name,
    To bless the world, to banish tyrant greed
        That dwarfs and crushes, to enlarge the day
        That lights man's footsteps on the upward way!

When men forget the deeds our heroes wrought,
  Immortal Lincoln's never-fading lines,
That melted with their touch of burning thought
    The bondman's fetters; when the land reclines
        In that soft ease that spurns the patriot's toil,
        Then demagogues may claim it as their spoil.

Then may the lust of power, the craze of greed,
  And anarchy that feeds her hungry hordes
On broken hearts, ride on with reckless speed
    Nor fear the avenging wrath of freedom's swords:
        But God be praised! the people stand erect
        And true and noble in their self-respect.

Their self-respect, their love for law, their zeal
  For this good government the fathers gave.
So much imbued with freedom each would feel
    Himself a slave, if the land held a slave·

For patriots are patriots first of all,
Alert to freedom's danger, instant to her call.

Republicans and Democrats are we,
   Or what you will for party; but as one
Strong unit, firm, united, earnest, free,
   Henceforth we stand for all our heroes won:
         One hope inspiring every sister State,
         One perfect union grandly free and great.

Each name that grateful Indiana writes
   On yonder pile she builds to hero fame,
Each gallant deed her history recites,
   Each word for him whose headstone bears no name,
         Shall teach the generations as they rise
         Our freedom's cost in blood and sacrifice.

And not alone to those who staked their lives
   Or fell in death, we build, for God was good
And gave us mothers, sisters, sweethearts, wives,
   Whose hearts were true through gathering tears and
         blood,
         Whose hands upheld the hands that fought and
            won,
         And crowned the brave men when their work
            was done.

O! mothers, sisters of our hero dead,
   O! ye who wept the unreturning brave,
Daughters or dearer ones, whose tears were shed
   As love's libations; ye were strong to save

The land we love! Long may your sainted
    names
Be history's treasure, freedom's trust and fame's.

We build to love, not hatred; every stone
  We consecrate unto a soldier's fame
Shall have a voice like Memnon's morning tone,
  And through the lapse of lapsing years proclaim
    Man's love for man in liberty's increase,
    And right's armistice which shall never cease.

For peace is only peace when men are free,
  Chains and oppression are relentless war;
The strong against the weak. The tyrant's glee
  Is but the shackle's clank. Hope's dawning star
    Smiles on red fields of storm and battle when
    Force crushes force that peace may reign again.

Lay deep and strong your corner-stone; build high
  The shaft that speaks of glory; let your love
Outsoar your deed, for lo! the day is nigh
  When the white-tented hosts that camp above,
    Shall claim the last brave man whose head of
      gray
    Sheds its warm lustre on the land today.

So shall you build, and may your building stand
  On sure foundations, sunk to nature's core;
May freedom's spirit rule the happy land
  And peace and knowledge grow from more to more;
    And when Time dies mid elemental wars
    May His last gaze be on the stripes and stars.

TO J. W. R.

On a Contemplated Visit To England.

Since you and I each unto each confessed
   Faint hope that fame might favor and with toil
      combine
  To bear our names beyond the county line,
You've conquered half the world, deserved the rest,
And now to England hasten, love possessed,
   To bow your Western manhood at the shrine
   Of Avon's bard, or where the gracious Nine
On Albion's Laureate their endowments pressed,
   Feel, in that air, how genius, art combine
   To weld in love our Anglo-Saxon line:
Or in sweet Scotia, by enchanted Ayr,
   Walk arm in arm with Burns's ghost and blend
   Your kindred soul with his, as friend with friend,
So may God prosper you and keep you in His care!

THE POET.

God made the poet,
  Nature wrought his heart;
But foolish fortune
  Heeded not his art.

Heaven wooed the boy
  To songs divinest skill,
But men and critics
  Joined to work him ill.

His plea for love
  The cruel heart denied;
His wail for bread
  Was silenced when he died.

But from his ashes
  There uprose a tree,
A brier, a vine,
  A flower to woo the bee:

And men and maidens
  Sought the happy bower
To dream sweet dreams
  Through many an idle hour.

They, listening, heard not
  But were still aware
Of rhyme and motion
  In the ambient air: —

A viewless presence,
  Palpitating, sweet,
That swayed their souls
  As zephyr sways the wheat

When quails are nesting,
  Till each man and maid
Discerned the poet
  Trembling through the shade.

The poet dies not
  Though the man depart,
Sweet mother nature
  Holds him in her heart,

Renews his singing
  Year by year and swells
Her aeons of bloom
  With his love miracles.

God made the poet,
  Nature wrought his heart,
But foolish fortune
  Heeded not his art,

And when she famished
  On her gilded crust,
The poet rose up singing
  From the dust.

IN SUMMER TIME.

To L. O. H. — True Poet and Gentleman.

In summer time, at flush of noon,
I love my discord, hate your tune;
I love your song, forget my rhyme,
At evening sweet in summer time.
I shout your song, forget my rhyme,
When birds and bees together chime,
At morning's blush in summer time.

THE PLODDER.

O, poet, my poet! on fancy's wing,
From your nest in the world to the worlds that
  gleam
In the astral depths of your cosmic dream
Upsoaring forever, the songs you sing, —
The thoughts that cluster about your way
Like sun-swept clouds at the gates of day, —
Come up from the low, sweet earth where toil
Is guardian and groom to the fruitful soil.

I am a plodder, and plodders know
The cool, glad spots where the lilies grow;
And while you float in your airs divine,
And rave of Apollo and chase the Nine,
Each blossom takes root in the good, green earth,
Each thought immortal has here its birth;
And here at the core and heart of things,
Toil is the minstrel that lords the strings
Of the myriad-echoing lute of life.
Here dreamers are vassals and plodders kings,
And the hero who wages eternal strife,
Not the child of fancy who floats and swings
On the air of an old, dead dream of things,
Is the master whose art has the condor wings.

And O, my poet! when you dig deep,
With dearth of leisure and loss of sleep,

When you plod with me, when you toil and moil
In thought's rough field, truth's bitter soil,
It is then you gain strength to soar on high;
From the sweat of toil build your rainbow road
Through the earth and the sky to the ged's abode.

I am the plodder, and day by day
I do my work in my humble way;
I banish the bramble and sow the corn,
Cherish the rose and destroy the thorn;
Conquer the savage, control the brute,
Invade the desert with flower and fruit;
Build your cities and sail your ships,
Compound your nectars for beauty's lips:
I feed the presses that hum and roar,
And gather the news from sea and shore.

I build the palace and dig the moat;
I fashion the noose for the murderer's throat;
I shape and chisel the Sphinx's face
Or weave the daintiest films of lace;
I tunnel the mountains and stretch the wire,
Direct the lightning, and steam and fire
Obey my will, as, by genius taught,
I plod my way in the steps of thought.

I was born of a thought, and yet I stand
A servant forever, at thought's command:
The violet blooms where my hand is laid
Or the temple stands fair by the banyan's shade.

You, poet, may sail on your ether wing,
But till I have a hand in the song you sing

It will kindle no smile, will provoke no tear,
And will fade and be lost as a leaf that is sear.

You walk with your head in the air, a god, •
While close to the grass and the mold I plod.
You see the earth under you from on high:
I look from the sod to the blessing sky.
You win, with my help, a fadeless name;
I chisel it deep in the temple of fame.

But fame and its temple shall fade away,
And names shall be lost as the dreams of a day;
Then poet and plodder together shall rest
Low cradled on Nature's compassionate breast;
But in heaven the plodder may sing, and the wise,
Happy poet rejoice in the toils of the skies.

THAT RARE OLD LAUGH.

Where is your happy laugh, comrade,
　　That used to ring so free?
Somehow, my old ears ache for it,
　　As I heard it in sixty-three;
But you smile on me such a mournful smile,
　　And chuckle so faint and low,
That your laugh is only the ghost of the laugh
　　That you laughed so long ago.

Your hair was black as the beetle's wing,
　　And your voice was brave and strong;
And whether the battle was fierce and wild,
　　Or the march was hard and long,
That old, rare laugh of yours would ring,
　　When a comrade needed cheer,
And shake the wrinkles of care out smooth,
　　With its echoes glad and clear.

When rations were short and springs were dry,
　　And our tongues were swollen, thick,
I've heard your cheery old laugh ring high,
　　And down on the double quick,
Along the lines ran a thrill of joy,
　　With answering laugh and shout;
For the boys caught on to the anchor, hope,
　　Whenever your laugh rang out.

Then ha, ha, ha! and ha, ha, ha!
　Hurrah for the days of old!
In the army time, in the soldier time,
　When hearts were true and bold.
We shed some tears for the men who fell,
　We moaned in our days of pain,
But your cheery laugh was a cordial rare,
　That was never poured in vain.

You laughed when you hobbled back to us,
　With crutch and bandage and sling,
"To harvest three wounds at once," you said,
　" Was a *wounderful* sort of thing."
I can hear you call when the ague froze,
　Or the fever burned your brow;
" It's no trick to be cool, no task to get warm,
　If you only just know how!"

But where has your old laugh gone, my lad,
　And why has it died away?
I knew that your form must be bent and old,
　And your hair and beard be gray,
But the old, rare laugh that you used to laugh,
　I had thought to hear ring out
From your dear old lips till my soul could stand
　Tiptoe on the hills and shout.

Subdued and saddened and softened down
　By the stress of our social ways,
Your laugh is timed to the steps of age,
　Not the marches of former days;
Its bugle calls to the double quick

Shall never be heard again;
'Tis now the treble of "Soldier's Rest,"
    Not the Marseillaise of men.

But let us remember the laughs of old,
    And remember the comrade strong,
And shake your old hand with a right good will,
    As we join in story and song;
For the war, and the boys, and the deeds will
        soon
    Be but memory, history, love,
But we'll be friends till the bugle sounds
    To join the ranks above.

And there, in that happy world, somewhere,
    Sometime, when the winds are low,
And we can hear back in the far-away,
    Sweet sounds that we used to know,
I think we shall hear your rare, old laugh
    Ring up o'er the golden bars
'Till we shall leap on the hills and shout
    "Three cheers for the stripes and stars."

THE DEMOCRACY OF TOIL.

I do not hold and I will not hold
That he who toils in the dust and mold
Is less than the owner of lands and gold,
Or bound, as a serf, in a righteous thrall
To come and to go at the usurer's call,
To bow to a master, to cringe and fawn
For the sake of the rags that his limbs have on.

One toils with the shovel and one with the pen,
And which is the greater or which more wise,
Let no man question, for what are men
To judge of the toils by which others rise?
For toil is forever the angel's wing
That raises the peasant, deposes the king
And gives us a man in his stead, the thing
That poets honor and thieves despise.

A poet may starve and deserve his death
For singing nought worth its cost in breath,
But he who teaches a rose to climb
Or wooes from the mold with a will sublime
The plumed and bannered delight of corn,
Is priest to nature, though peasant born,
As toiling with sun and mist and morn
And the heat of noon and the evening's breath
He bringeth life from the dust of death,
And winneth from thistle and weed and thorn
And savage squalor and feudal scorn,
A world of beauty, a world of grace,

A warm, sweet world with a smiling face,
To mirror faintly some tender line
Of benignant joy from the face divine.

A poet may starve and deserve his death
For singing nought worth its cost in breath,
A monarch may die for his country's good,
A demagogue sink in the waste of mud
His cunning expands for the feet of men,
But an honest toiler with brawn or pen,
At forge in forest, on land or main,
Has ever the key to the truest gain,
The gain that develops, or gain enwrought
On the gain of growth by the growth of thought.

I do not hold and I will not hold,
That this swart toiler, by need controlled,
Must trot forever with head bowed down
At the chariot tail as the lordly clown,
Or, lord by accident, drives away
To the plaudits of fools who hope, some day,
To task their fellows that self same way:
For lord by title or lord by gain,
Or lord by lineage, or lord by might;
American lord by oil or grain,
By wreck of railroad, disdain of right;
Or little lord in some country place
By legalized thefts that would thieves disgrace,
Usurious lordling with soul to crave
The pennies that pay for the poor man's grave,
I care not whence the white-washed fraud
Receives its sanction to mock at God,

I do not hold and I will not hold
That, by its crime of dishonest gold
Such lordship stands in a nobler stead
Than simple manhood that toils for bread.

The world may laugh, but I still must hold
That vulgar pride which is born of gold,
Yet not of gold, for the ore is pure,
But of power it gives to oppress the poor,
To flaunt and flutter and override,
And to put on airs that were else denied,
Is cruel as death and hard as fate
To bind, to oppress, to desolate.
I would not rage and I would not rend,
Nor hasten in tears and blood the end:
But the end will come, and the human heart
That has quivered so long in the Godless mart,
Will rise up whole, and the toiler's toil
Shall be honored more than the rich man's spoil,
And the gilded clown shall be only —a clown,
And the man be up and the brute be down.

And so I repeat and repeat again,
Though standing, perhaps, as one to ten,
That I do not hold and I will not hold,
That he who toils in the dust and mold,
Is less than the owner of lands and gold,
Or bound as a serf, in a righteous thrall,
To come and to go at the usurer's call,
To bow to a master, or cringe and fawn
For the sake of the rags that his limbs have on.

THE LAND OF FIRST LOVE.

There silence is music,
And rest is rejoicing,
And being is ecstasy
    Sweeter than morning,
When corn blades in whispers
Are tenderly voicing
The soul of the sunshine
    That tremblingly wooes them.

There vows of the ages
Are gathered and blended
To one murmuring spirit,
    One echo melodious,
As freed from all passion
The notes had descended
From heaven in dreamy,
    Delirious pulsations.

There sounds not the Swan Song,
The song of the dying,
For hope is enchanter,
    And life is immortal;
And all the sweet languors
That ever went sighing
Through amorous springtimes,
    Are centered and softened.

There, sweeter than pinks
Or the breath of wild roses,
A balm floateth in
    From the sea-girdled islands, —
A wind of the morning,
Where beauty reposes
And veils her fair face
    In the light of her tresses.

O, land of all lands!
There are songs in thy fountains,
And raptures untold
    In thy bloom-lighted meadows,
While Muses divine
Still inhabit thy mountains,
And Pan leads his shepherds
    And flocks by thy rivers.

Thy people are dreamers
Whose lives are enchanted.
Like Memnon of old,
    All thy rocks utter music,
And all of thy castles
And gardens are haunted
By spirits that float
    In the palpitant starlight.

There mortals have wings
And are mortals no longer:
At sunset and moonrise
    Tall seraphs, fair angels,
Lock hands and glide onward,

While love waxeth stronger,
And sweetly delirious
   They rave in their heaven.

O life and O love!
What is youth in its gladness
Till once in this land
   It has dreamed and run riot?
If waking be sorrow,
Or mating be madness,
There's joy in the mem'ry
   Of love and its longing.

.

THE OLD BLAZED ROAD.

The old blazed road, it wound and wound,
  Through the depths of the forest dark and dim,
Where the last year's leaves gave a muffled sound
  Under the horse-shoe's iron rim;

Over the hill by the wand'ring brook,
  Down where the buttonwood copses grew
And the frogs were loud; by the smiling nook
  Where the parted oaks let the sunshine through.

Wandering on in its lonesome way
  By fragrant tangle and drift-choked stream;
From the far-off village, a struggling ray
  Shot into the wild wood's savage-dream.

And brave and true were the men who rode
  Deep into the wilderness long ago,
And scored the trees for the old blazed road
  For the settlers to follow, and following so

To come with their wives and their worldly gear —
  Small worth had the gear, hope made it great —
To love, to labor, to plant, to rear
  A solid base for the future State.

There were happy journeys, on summer days,
  And songs and joy in the winters grim;
The lay of love and the chant of praise,
  The warrior's lyric, the Christian's hymn.

And many a bridal cavalcade
  Has graced its windings, as two by two,
The backwoods lad and the backwoods maid
  With laughter ringing the forests through

Frightened the deer from his noonday lair,
  Scared off the fox to his gloomy den,
And ruffled the tempers of wolf and bear,
  Or echoed the catamount's scream again.

And O, for the sorrow! and O, for the tears!
  As the little plank coffin went on before,
Borne in the patriarch's arms, whose years
  Were rich in sympathy's garnered store.

For the funeral march as the bridal train,
  Was known full well to the ancient trace.
When death reaped blossom as well as grain,
  Tears followed smiles on the settler's face:

Tears followed smiles, and the old blazed road
  Faded and faded as forests fell,
Till now where once the latch string showed
  A warmth of welcome no words can tell

In the settler's cabin, the rich man's home,
  Stands fair and stately in garden lawn,
And the trains sweep by, and the people come,
  But the backwoods world is forever gone.

Forever gone with its rude old ways,
  Its heartfelt sorrows, its lusty joys,

Its restful nights and its toilsome days,
  Its home-spun lassies and bare-foot boys.

But long shall the lover of nature dream,
  Of the wild, dim path where the spices blew
Their breath of fragrance by swamp and stream,
  And the red buds flamed when the spring was
    new.

When the soul of the forest went into the soul
  And sweetened the life with its wild-wood sweets,
When manners were cordial and costumes droll,
  And hates were not hidden by smooth deceits.

For haters were haters and men were men,
  And women were fickle and women were true,
And lovers were lovers and jealous, then,
  And cooed and quarrelled as lovers do.

The scars on the trees to the left and right
  Went beckoning into the forests grand,
And those who had courage to win the fight,
  Followed and conquered and tamed the land:

Followed and conquered, and still we dream,
  And backward gaze where the ancient trace
Wound under the willows and through the stream,
  A wandering rhythm of matchless grace.

It was good to live in that early time,
  To laugh and to weep by the forest road,
To toil and struggle, to crawl or climb,
  And carry forward one's daily load.

It is better to live in this better day; —
  As part of the present, to move and thrill
To its onward motion and pulse and play,
  And true to the new, to the old true still,

Move forward, forward with ceaseless quest
  For all good things by the Lord bestowed,
Till we enter at last to the perfect rest
  That lies at the end of the well-blazed road.

AFTER DECORATION.

The crowds are gone, the wreaths lie withering,
The hymns are hushed and darkness and the dead
Are mute companions where were lately shed
The tears of women and the flowers of spring.
O! tears and flowers and eloquence that bring
That dreadful past back on love's wounded wing,
And lead us where our heroes fought and bled,
Ye faint and fail as fails each transient thing:
But each old mother following back the thread
Of quickened memory to the curly head
She pillowed on her bosom ere she read
Of war and tumult in the land, or said
"Go forth, my son!" speaks through her tears
　　again,
The Nation still needs mothers to bequeath it men.

ON GROWING OLD.

O, sing to me the gladness
  Of spring's rejoicing song,
Or love's delightful measures
  When summer days are long!

The ebb-tide moves not slowly,
  But still our souls delay,
To catch the latest sunshine
  Of youth's receding day.

We shrink from yonder darkness
  And waste of pathless main,
And list each shore-line murmur
  Of far-off youth's refrain.

In some far, sheltered harbor,
  When o'er the heavenly wall,
On eyes grown tired with longing,
  A sweeter light shall fall,

Shall not the storm-tossed vessel
  Cast anchor, safe at last,
And there the weary spirit
  Renew its happy past?

O! if for one brief moment
  That joy to me be given,
'Twill sweeten ever after
  The sweetest joys of heaven.

THE WEIRS — 1890.

Fair Winnepisaukee, I pass by thy shore,
And I see the white wings of the gulls and the boats,
And the wandering delirium of sunlight and shade
That across thy glad waters enchantingly floats,
And up from the islands, like rapture conveyed
On the glances of beauty when lovers adore,
Flieth smiling aloft till the mountains, arrayed
In that tremulous marvel of shadow and light,
Seem tenderly veiling their own rugged might.

O, Winnepisaukee! Sweet lake of the hills!
As fair as Killarney, as wild Loch Achray
Romantic and glad, — there are songs in thy waves
Like the music of horns, there are echoes that play
Like the voices that flow from Æolian caves
When the wind of the evening its spirit distils
With the dew and the odor of roses that laves
Every sense in delight, till we cry in sweet pain
With the joy of a thought that no words can retain.

O, Winnepisaukee! the Great Spirit's smile!
I shall see thee in mem'ry, renew thee in dreams
When the tides of sweet June gallop in on the wheat,
And the green herons call to their mates by the
        streams;
And thy Islands shall cry and thy mountains repeat
In my soul to my soul through each long, weary mile
Of the journey I take, and thy waves kiss my feet
And thy beauty inspire me, give words to my tongue
And thy gladness conspire still to keep the heart young.

THE LESSON OF THE GRASS.

The grass that underneath the snow
  Sends forth its shoots of tender green,
Recks not though threat'nirg clouds hang low,
  And winds are loud and frosts are keen;
For upward through its roots there steals
A quickening influence that reveals
The slow-paced summer stealing on —
In outline faint as some far dawn.

And so the grass renews its hold
  And lifts its manifold sweet stems
And spreads faint verdure on the mold
  Along the orchard's sunlit hems;
For it perceives the secret sweet
That lifts the heart and speeds the feet
And thrills the soul of man or bird
With truth no mortal ear has heard.

What is this subtle sense that wakes
  The pulses in the tender root,
Or warns the grass when winter breaks,
  Or thrills the mandrake's hidden shoot?
And wherefore do the woods and fields
Begin to smile as winter yields,
Ere yet the vernal breezes rise
To warm the earth and paint the skies?

And wherefore does the weary heart,
  So long depressed with doubt and gloom,
Leap up again with sudden start
  As some waked Lazarus from the tomb?
And love so long a silent shade,
Why should it quicken and invade
The half-roused soul, and make it sing
As dawn's bird, head still under wing?

I only know but this — the thought
  Of God or Nature, what you will, —
The power is all, the name is naught, —
  Seems every haunt of life to fill
With knowledge, impulse, hope, desire,
The pulse to quicken, thrill, inspire;
To swell the bud, expand the leaf,
Beget the lover's sweet belief,

And link all things to life and light,
  And warmth of suns and wealth of soils,
And growth and verdure that delight
  To hide the grim destroyer's spoils,
Provoking even from foul decay
New graces for the rising day,
And from love's loss renewing love,
Life conquering death at each remove.

And so I view the passing years
  And see the seasons come and go,
Sometimes in smiles, sometimes in tears,
  And dimly still through pulse and flow

Of all this many-mysteried stream
That we call nature, catch the gleam
Of some diviner life, the glow
Of heaven within the life we know, —

God's presence in this mortal frame,
 His thought alike in flower or star,
His genius in the morning's flame,
 His soul where brooks and lilies are;
In worlds or systems, suns or seeds,
On Calvary's cross; where Cato bleeds,
In life or death, in growth, decay ; —
And all I know I sing and say,

That closer than we think or dream
 The larger world about us lies,
With life that is life's source, the stream
 Whose waters quicken paradise.
Howe'er we doubt it bideth near
 And wooes us ever; though we fear
Its awful presence, still it rests
 A peaceful dweller in our breasts.

If force is blind and has no care
 For loss or suffering, pain or grief,
As sombre pessimists declare,
 Shall that destroy our sweet belief
That here or there, or far or near,
 Life holds us in an atmosphere
Of love divine, serene, intense,
 That heeds no point of time or sense,

And from our fading clay unfolds
  The fadeless spirit's trembling wing,
And through the eternal years upholds
  Love, joy and heaven and everything
Wherein, wherewith the soul may gain
  Its mastery over grief and pain?
If this be foolish, fools are wise
  To trust the love such seers despise.

WRITTEN IN AN ALBUM

You ask for a rhyme in this book of yours:
  A rhyme, fair maiden, of what shall it be?
Shall it speak the struggle that long endures;
  For the fame that liveth eternally?
Ah no, my maiden, fame comes too high
  And wreathes but heads that are growing gray:
Better by far, as the years go by,
  A joy that is steadfast day by day,
With a laugh to laugh and a song to sing,
  And a hope forever blossoming.

THOMAS M. BROWNE.

In Memoriam.

Whom genius blest, and honor crowned with bays,
And love rewarded with her sacred trust,
Untouched by blame, unflushed by kindly praise,
He lies at rest low in our kindred dust.
How frail is man; how fleeting honor's breath!
But kindly thought and noble deed remain
To lift our friend above the mold of death,
In that long life of human hope and gain,
Wherein, wherefrom the statesman never dies,
Who lives for man, for liberty is wise.

O, friend of many years! we come not now
With long-drawn sighs to moan above thy rest.
Life's work well done, a victor crowned art thou,
With freedom's faithful few forever blest.
Wherefore we call to thee across the line,
"Hail and farewell;" farewell and sweetest hail!
The history made, the guerdons won are thine,
And ours the influence that shall never fail,
The long endeavor, the unbroken will,
The courage dauntless in the face of ill.

He came to us unfriended in his youth;
For him no college reared its friendly wall;
He heard, far off, the rallying cry of truth;
Half understood, full trusted that high call;

And so through toil and penury he wrought
His way to knowledge, purpose, influence, place
In that domain whose conqueror is thought,
Whose wealth is wisdom schooled in honor's ways.
Let youth take heart of hope since those prevail,
Who strive with courage, while the halting fail.

Alike undaunted, 'mid the battle's roar,
Or in the forum when the storm was loud
Of angry factions, the white plume he wore
Shone like an oriflamme above the cloud.
No coward fears beset his onward way:
For man, for country, for the toiler's right
He wrought through years of doubt, and when the
          day
Of broader freedom rose with clearer light,
He did not in the auroral splendor pause,
But strove for wiser measures, better laws.

Sleep, statesman, soldier, comrade, neighbor, friend!
Thy well-earned rest no battle cry shall break.
Above thy dust the thoughtful people bend,
With many offerings wrought for love's dear sake.
Here let the freedman's happy children meet
And shout their gladness; let the aspiring boy
Who treads a thorny path with bleeding feet,
Take courage here and thrill with hope and joy!
The spot that holds our Tom Browne's honored
          clay,
Is doubly sacred soil to such as they.

As one by one are quenched the hero's lights,
Their last tattooes are sounded, and the stars
Look down in peace from their celestial heights,
While mercy veils the fiery front of Mars,
May the sweet silence where they sleep be filled
With freedom's presence, and the vital air
With patriot faith and energies be thrilled,
To purge the world of slavery, want, despair!
And so farewell, wise leader — noble friend!
Like heaven for thee, our love shall have no end.

THE BARD OF THE PEOPLE

There once was a singer in Scotland,
  A bard of the fields and the streams;
A poet of love and love's longing,
  A dreamer of wonderful dreams.
He sang at the plow tail, he sweetened
  With music his sorrowful crust.
He poured his soul out in libation
  To an age that was hard and unjust.

He saw man in honor uprising
  O'er caste and the pride of renown;
He lashed the dull hypocrite's folly
  And laughed at the dogmatist's frown,
Then stooped to weep over the daisy
  His plowshare upturned with the sod,
And with the good cotter at evening
  Sent up his thanksgiving to God.

He died when the clouds gathered darkly,
  And skies were all hidden from view,
But yonder in fame's constellation
  His star shineth full in the blue:
The poet of peasant and lassie,
  The bard of the love-stricken heart,
His songs like his themes are immortal
  And fadeless and faultless as art.

And still rides the *fou* Tam O'Shanter
  Through ages of darkness and storm,
And love, the perennial enchanter,
  Renews every feature and form—
Sweet Mary, dear Jean, all that haunted
  Blithe Ayre with the soul of Lang Syne,
Or cherished this bard of the people
  And rendered his singing divine.

THE MOSSES.

To Don L. Paine, after reading his dainty little volume of poems entitled Club Moss.

As rare and fine as love's design
  Of beauty wrought on cupid's wing,
Where gently low the breezes blow
  And wildly sweet the thrushes sing;
On shadowed mold of forests old
  The mosses lift their tiny bells.
Or spread their carpets, green and gold,
  In nooks of boulder-haunted dells.

Joy of the earth that gave them birth,
  True children of the soil are they;
What else were bare, their love and care
  Make beautiful and glad alway.
Their dainty stems are crowned with gems,
  Fit splendors for a fairy queen,
And beech roots gray, where squirrels play,
  They lightly bind in verdant sheen.

On rotten roofs they spread their woofs,
  And hide in smiles their slow decay;
O'er crumbling walls their gladness falls
  And crowns dim rocks with hoods of gray.
They love to run where shade and sun
  Eclipse each other in swift change,
At meadow side where lizards glide
  And elms their sturdy pickets range.

They woo the breeze, they love the trees,
　And when they fall, with tender care
Wrap soft and deep their lowly sleep
　In plushes rich and velvets rare,
Whereon recline the sacred Nine,
　And lovers coo and poets wait;
And hearts are won and webs are spun,
　And snails are born and ants debate.

O, mosses sweet! my idle feet
　Have often sought your haunted nooks,
And made aware that spirits fare
　Within your realm as thought in books,
Souls in perfume or song in bloom,
　Or love where April violets spring,
Have striven in vain to catch one strain
　Of any happy song they sing.

But here Dan Paine, — God give him gain
　Of all glad witcheries that inspire! —
Has caught and wound to rhythmic sound,
　Such notes from many a spirit lyre.
He heard them low where mosses grow
　And brooks and birds their lays repeat;
He wrought them well, and truth to tell
　Moss roses ne'er were half so sweet.

THE SHOUT OF AN OPTIMIST.

Once I hung my harp in sorrow
  On the willow branches, crying
"Love and song have no tomorrow!
  Song and love and hope are dying:
Puny critics, lying censors,
  Lives that move but to the jingle
Of the dollar; rhyme dispensers
  Who with amorous measures mingle
Hints of lustful, loveless passions
  Till love dieth in the waking
And the few fond hearts it fashions
  Are esteemed but fit for breaking!"

Hot with childish indignation,
  "These," I cried, "our modern leaders,
Hail with shout and salutation;
  Give them followers, give them readers;
Pour your gold into their coffers,
  Wave your night-shade garlands o'er them;
Seize the blossomed bough love offers,
  Tread it under foot before them:
Drive your poets forth in sorrow,
  While your rhymesters mock their crying,
'Song and love have no tomorrow,
  Love and song and hope are dying!'"

Yet again, O, breath of morning!
  I perceive thy cooling kisses,
Thrilling me with subtle warning
  That such lovely world as this is
Must be consecrate forever
  To the higher and the better;
That each age has some strong lever
  Wherewith man shall break a fetter
That benumbs him and enthralls him,
  Till some thought-born revelation,
Like a far-off trumpet, calls him,
  To his sunward destination.

Then I pause and think, remember —
  Love and song and hope grow weary
Gazing on some fading ember
  Of a fire that once burned clearly; —
As the ember fades in ashes,
  Lo! across the heaven is streaming
Larger light that moves and flashes
  With an ultimate far gleaming
Into lower depths of sorrow,
  Into nights before unlighted:
Then I shout and call — "Tomorrow,
  Shall a million wrongs be righted!"

Come then, harp! there are no willows
  Worthy thee as are these fingers:
Not for thee the swaying pillows
  Of the dallying wind that lingers

With the sweet-souled summer weather
  On the idle string neglected;
Thou and I must toil together,
  Brave and strong and undejected.
Should our rude notes be unheeded
  And our loves be food for laughter,
Yet our trembling songs are needed
  For the sum of the hereafter.

Hail, O, prophets, poets, sages!
  Through the ages calling, crying;
On your heaven-illumined pages
  Cent'ring energies undying!
Leave, small bardlings, your oblivion,
  Ye with meaner singing quickened
Humblest souls in night's dominion
  Where the shades converged and thickened.
Poets, lovers, all the air is
  Pregnant with your souls victorious,
From the bard of our Sierras
  Back to Homer, blind and glorious.

None may fail the heavens that call him
  And be more than Mammon's creature:
Ease may fly and woe befall him,
  Grief may darken every feature,
Yet with strong and high devotion
  To the wiser, better, sweeter,
Deeper tides in thought's vast ocean,
  He shall know his life completer,
And with sunward hope unfailing,

Where the myriad barks are thronging,
He shall set his shallop sailing
  To the shores of love's far longing.

He who gives is blest in giving,
  Though the gift be small in measure,
If its thought possess the living,
  Fadeless wealth of love's rich treasure,—
Love that maketh man immortal,
  Love that on his Atlas shoulders
Bears the worlds, and at life's portal
  In thought's crude beginning smoulders
As a fire that may hereafter
  Light the heavens with its far gleaming;
Love that laughs the truest laughter,
  And is sacred even in dreaming.

Wherefore poets, toilers, sages,
  Men who delve the earth, or soaring
O'er Olympus, storm the ages,
  Hear the souls of men imploring—
"Spare no genius, gift, invention,
  Spare no humble toil nor labor,
Song that echoes love's intention—
  Hope to man and help to neighbor, · ·
Hope and help, the Christ in spirit,
  Help and hope, the Buddha's teaching,
Help, to win life's crown of merit,
  Hope, whose wisdom is best preaching!"

Heed, O, Optimists! this crying,
  And let not your gifts lie rusting,

All their strength to man denying, –
  Man the blind, the struggling, trusting,
Crushed by greed and superstition,
  Pride of caste and rank and station,
Dwarfed by ignorance, inanition,
  Sins inherited, starvation, —
Mind and spirit. Hear, and heeding
  Rise from ease's lethean pillows
And with faith to join love's pleading
  Take your harps down from the willows.

Yet, be sure of this, my singer,
  Noise is vain and art is fleeting,
And e'en song shall fail to linger
  Here where shades and myths retreating,
Backward hurl their dark inventions;
  If it have not soul and measure
Warmed by love's divine contentions,
  If it hold not some rich treasure
For the babes of the hereafter,
  Some glad influence, some red letter
Touch of pathos or sweet laughter
  To inspire and make men better.

TO COATES KINNEY.

On reading Pessim and Optim.

Art thou descended from the sea kings old?
  Or wherefore hear we thundering through thy song
The voice of seas that will not be consoled,
  But cry and murmur, as the ages throng,
To stormy capes, green islands, sunless caves,
  To wonder worlds that lie beneath the waves?

Thy printed page suggests the book unwrought,
  Thy song presages sweeter song to be
In some deep future, and thy lightest thought
  Flows like the tide upon the summer sea,
Or when love claims it for his sweet behoof,
  Falls pattering with "the rain upon the roof."

Sing on, wise bard! Turn Pessim out to grass
  And let glad Optim lead your onward way;
Though men may utter as you singing pass
  The old Greek's cry, "Why crown a head that's
      gray?"
Such silvered head is for the poet's crown.
  Stars may be splendid when the sun is down;

And when, at last — long hence our love insists —
  Your sun flames down the west and out of sight,
Our little bards whose songs are vocal mists
  Of faith, hope, music, melody, delight,
May rise and smile with light for ages far
  And each be deemed a happy morning star.

MY LITTLE BROTHER.

I remember the dear little boy,
    With the seven sweet years in his heart,
Brief Aprils of sorrow and joy,
    For his life of my life was a part.

So tender and brave and true,
    Child and man in desire and pursuit,
April bloom in the morning's dew
    With the flavor of ripened fruit.

Wisdom is sweet in a child
    When it comes in an artless way,
And is modest and undefiled
    By the pride of our haughty clay.

You could hear in his quiet words
    More than your scholars know,
And the warble of happy birds
    Was his laughter's undertow.

He was nature's own and mine
    And our mother's darling pet,
But the seal of a love divine
    On his little brow was set;

And we saw and did not see,
    And we knew and did not know
That his kindred with bird and bee
    And the winds that whisper low,

Was the sign of a fleeting life,
  Like a rapture, a dream, a tone,
Or a prayer that stilleth strife,
  Then leaveth the heart alone.

Out of heaven there came a cry,
  And our dull ears heard it not,
Through the maples a moan went by,
  Grief entered our lowly cot.

That was years and years ago,
  Yet I see his pale, sweet face
And I rock him to and fro
  And hold him in my embrace.

Wisdom and sweetest light
  And love and the love of joy,
Went out of my arms that night
  With the soul of that little boy

But after he went away
  And left us a dower of grief,
There grew in us every day
  The flower of a sweet belief, —

Bud and blossom and leaf
  Full from the tender shoot,
And we wait —for the days are brief —
  For the blush of the ripened fruit.

We wait, and his thought returns
  With his humor's sparkling play,

And the soul within me yearns
  For the things he used to say.

I smile at some odd conceit,
  Some quaint, remembered whim,
And my heart and eyes repeat
  The tenderness learned from him.

He was only a little child
  Who lived his little years,
Who cried, but more often smiled,
  And went out in a rain of tears,

Yet he liveth in all things sweet
  That I either hear or see;
In the violet at my feet,
  In the flight of bird or bee;

In the ring of the poet's rhyme,
  In the tender joy of song,
In the flush of the summer time
  When the days are fair and long.

In the shout of my stalwart boy,
  In wife and daughters and home,
In the pathos of grief or joy,
  In the hope for joys to come.

There is naught that is good and fair
  That my brother dwells not in,
And he holds me from despair
  And wooes me away from sin.

He and his sister sweet,
  Serene as the summer skies,
From some divine retreat
  In their holy paradise,

Seem ever to watch and call,
  With a longing that will not cease,
To hold me in love's dear thrall
  To the hope of eternal peace.

It may be a mem'ry, a dream
  Wrought of past joy and grief,
A thing that doth only seem,
  A figment of old belief.

Be it so! if you will, but I
  Feel it blessing and peace to be
In the Eden of days gone by
  When they were as one with me.

And therefore it seemeth meet
  That in all things good and fair,
My brother and sister sweet
  Are my wardens everywhere.

BREAK, SAD HEART

Break, break! weak heart!
  Hard heart, so sad and cold!
  Days, years go by and joys are manifold;
And yet thou hidest, with a stupid art,
  Thy daily bliss and delvest in the mold
Of selfish sorrows; thy diviner part
  Holding itself as slave to fame or gold.
        Break! restless heart!
  So sad and hard, unsatisfied and cold!

Break, break, sad heart!
  And breaking break the thongs
  That bind thee to a thousand slavish wrongs;
To cruel creeds and selfish greeds that part
  Our little lives from the diviner throngs
Of heavenly messengers, whose daily art
  Each little joy in greater joy prolongs.
        Break, weary heart!
  And break the burden of thy many wrongs!

Yet, break not, heart!
  For broken hearts must fail!
  Whole-souled are they who over ill prevail
And yield no good to disappointment's smart,
  But struggle sunward even when foes assail,
And hold themselves alike in church or mart
  Prophets of hope and bearers of love's grail.
        Be strong, O heart!
  And by thy strength in weakness, still prevail.

Be strong, O, heart!
　But let thy foolish pride
　And greed be broken, lay thy hates aside,
Or trample them beneath thy feet and part
　From vain ambitions that are best denied,
And find in every spot some gentle art
　To woo thee as a lover woos his bride
And give thee peace, poor, weary, aching heart!
　　　Fond, foolish heart!
　Seek daily blessing and be satisfied.

THE HOUSE NOT MADE WITH HANDS.

Within, without this mortal shell
    That faints and falls as shadows fade,
The real house in which we dwell
    Lifts up its towers in sun or shade;
In sun or shade, in heat or cold,
    By native groves, on foreign strands,
We seek contentment, love — consoled,
    In this dear house not made with hands.

I know not where its porches end,
    I reck not that its turrets rise
From sure foundations, till they blend
    With the far cities of the skies;
How wide its walls, how large its halls,
    No thought within me understands,
Nor whence the healing shadow falls
    On this fair house not made with hands.

No seas so wide, no caves so deep,
    No path so lone, no crowd so great,
But safe the earnest soul may keep
    Its home enjoyments, simple state;
Its far, sweet yearnings, sweeter faith,
    Its treasures from all climes, all lands,
All regions known to life or death,
    Within our house not made with hands.

Its walls out-measure time and space,
    Or narrow to a closet's girth,
Hold heaven and hell in their embrace
    Or only one poor clod of earth.
They shut us close and hold us fast
    When self adored and sov'reign stands,
Till pining to be free, at last,
    Even from our house not made with hands,

We tread self down, touch hands and kiss
    With that far greater self that knows
Itself akin to all that is;—
    All life, all action, all repose;
Our visions widen then, the walls,—
    Winged walls—expand as day expands,
And we, whole-hearted, tread the halls
    Of our great house not made with hands.

Our house not made by mortal pains
    Hath deep foundations in the core
And heart of things, nor storms nor rains,
    Nor earthquake shocks, nor fires that pour
Their molten rocks in boiling seas
    Disturb its walls: sublime it stands
And offers shelter, rest and peace,—
    Our fadeless house not made with hands.

In what far ages old and dim
    In crusts of steaming worlds that late
Had sung in fire their morning hymn,
    When matter first grew constellate,

Our house was planned, its purpose wrought
   And shapen on life's primal sands,
Evades the quest of prying thought
   In this wide house not made with hands.

"Eternal in the heavens," 'tis said,
   Eternal in the eternal now,
We answer, and the happy dead
   Call back the answer. Where or how
Its walls are bounded, why they swell
   Or shrink about us like strong bands,
We know not; know but this, we dwell
   Within a house not made with hands.

Oh, blessed house not made with hands!
   Enriched by all that man has won
On stormy seas, on smiling lands,
   By all the sweetness of the sun;
Engarnitured by things divine;
   Diviner than love understands,
Past, present, future, all combine
   To bless our house not made with hands.

All evolutions, all estates,
   All thought, all wisdom, all desire,
Are one within its crystal gates,
   For him who from Promethean fire
Has caught the glow that warms and thrills,
   Sets life in motion and expands
Love's sweet ambition till it fills
   This boundless house not made with hands.

The faded æons on its walls
  In pictured glory reappear,
The far prophetic future calls
  In every note that wakes the ear
To sweetest music, or the low,
  Soft breezes murmur that commands
All vagrant fancies as they flow
  In this our home not made with hands.

Not made with hands, unwrought by toil,
  And wide as love's immortal arms;
Shall men who dig and men who moil
  For greed of gold that only harms,
Or greed of lust that blights and slays,
  Or greed of power, till spent as brands
In furnace fires, renew their days
  Safe in the house not made with hands?

Vain question! since each soul must dwell
  In its own mansion, foul or fair.
Though days return not, judge we well
  That pain is endless, and despair
Eternal to the trembling soul
  That in the darkened chamber stands?
Sometime, somewhere, the light may roll,
  Through all the house not made with hands.

Our mansions are prepared for us,
  Not we for them, but in them, lo!
This house was, is, shall be, and thus
  Life, birth, enjoyment, death, grief, woe,

Are all within and not without;
  No fierce *gensd'armes*, with rude commands,
May hurl the poor house-keeper out
  From this dear home not made with hands.

Ah, me! how crude and tame the words
  With which thought struggles after thought;
The babblement of brooks and birds,
  That seems but music meaning nought,
Exceeds us often when we fain
  Would only tread thought's border lands
And hear the eternal sea's refrain
  Pulse through the house not made with hands.

Perhaps hereafter men shall hear
  And feel and see where we are blind
And deaf and numb, and thought shall sphere
  Itself to knowledge unconfined
By time's environment, sin's thrall,
  Till ev'n the earth-bound soul commands
Some measure of the all in all —
  The fadeless house not made with hands.

But we whose narrow visions fail,
  Who grope and guess and walk by faith;
Who only through our love prevail
  O'er hourly anguish, daily death;
To us this yearning thought is sweet —
  Our house immortal is and stands
Where life's full fruit and promise meet —
  A Heavenly house not made with hands.

O, NAKED SOUL!

O, naked soul! bereft of each disguise,
  Each flattering pretense wherewith thou didst hide
Thy many frailties from thy own weak eyes,
  Torn from thee, e'en the friendly night denied
And the white light thrown on thy nakedness;
  Thy nakedness, thy wounds, thy selfish stains;
What sorrows rend thee and what dire distress
  Of torturing fears augment thy many pains!

O, naked soul! 'tis in thy nakedness
  That thou shalt know God with thee and at hand,
The searching gaze which needs that none confess
  That He should see and feel and understand:
And in thy nakedness alone, alone,—
  Whereat thy eyes must weep, thy tears arise —
Can thy own needs unto thyself be known,
  And hate be hateful even in honor's guise.

Away with every subterfuge, away
  With every ceremony, every right
That seeks to parry e'en the fiercest ray
  Of God's all-searching, all-revealing light!
Bid science delve and let the poet soar,
  Bid truth escape from ancient myths and be
The faithful mirror of all things, the lore
  Of past and present, time, eternity!

O, naked soul! forget thy coward fears!
  The light but loves thee, it shall hold thee fast,
And sweet'ning thee, perhaps, by many tears,
  Reveal thee to thyself so cleansed at last
That thou shalt draw to Nature's mother breast
  And weep thy ecstasy upon her heart,
And cradled there, as some sweet child at rest,
  Smile with the day and with the day depart.

TO THE SURVIVORS OF THE THIRTY-SIXTH
INDIANA VOLUNTEERS.

On being made an honorary member of their Regimental Association.

This is a real honor. Soldiers, heroes, friends,
  To be linked with you, hand and heart,
  You men of peace, who chose the part
Of combat for the right; whose history blends
  With liberty's; who learned not war's dread art
  For hate or conquest; you whose deeds impart
Their lustre to the State; whose love ascends
  At Freedom's shrine forever. This to me
  Is more than honor; for tonight I see
Sweeping again your full batallion line —
A thousand heroes with but one design —
  To that long march whence many came no more;
  And hail your glad return, when o'er
Your tattered colors Fame had written her sign.

THE COMING OF WINTER.

The leaf from the maple bough is blown
   And the white flower from the thorn;
And what shall we do when the night has flown
   And the clouds hang low at morn?

But yesterday were the meadows green,
   Tonight they are white with snow,
And the cattle crowd, for the winds are keen,
   Where the straw ricks stand a-row.

Good bye, good bye! to the robin's song
   And the mock-bird's checkered lay;
The frozen road will be rough and long
   And some may fall by the way.

We'll gather us close to the ingle side,
   While story and song abound,
And bloom shall safe in the bud abide
   Till the birds and the spring come round.

And who'll be gone, and who'll be here
   To see the lilies born,
When leaves on the maple bough appear
   And white flowers on the thorn?

* A COLLOQUY.

*(This dialogue derives its interest from the excellence of the answers, which
are by Lee O. Harris, who has kindly consented to their
use in this volume.)*

QUESTION.

Can you tell me, old man, why our hearts are still
    light,
  And to gladness and song we incline?
I thought men grew old when their heads became
    white
  And their souls then discarded the Nine.

                              — P.

REPLY.

If the heart hath a song when its spring time appears,
  And it yield to the Muse's control,
Why should it be mute when the Autumn of years
  Hath ripened the fruit of the soul?

The hand of the minstrel may tremble with age,
  And his harp may be sadly unstrung,
But memory tenderly turneth the page
  And the music forever is young.

                              — H.

QUESTION.

Can you tell why it is that the fields are more green,
  And the flowers gain in beauty each year?

*Written for and read at the annual meeting of the Western Association of Writers, in 1890.

I can't make it out, but full, calm and serene,
  I acknowledge this truth, with a tear,

That as pride falls away and old fallacies fade,
  And ambition sinks low in the dust,
Love maketh us bold where we once were afraid,
  And our doubts are but shadows of trust.
                                        — P.

REPLY.

On the pathway we tread, while the passions endure,
  Lieth dust from our hurrying feet;
But the rain-drops of sorrow can render it pure;
  Then the fields and the flowers grow sweet.

We pass from the brambles ambition hath strewn,
  And the roses of pride shall decay,
But low in the vale where we journey, are sown
  The lilies of love by the way.

Ambition and pride, like a story long told,
  Shall fade as the passions grow chill;
But the love and the song, they can never be old,
  Till the heart of the minstrel is still.
                                        — H.

SONG OF THE DEW DROP.

I am a drop of dew
  Soiled on the dusty leaf;
Shadowed and trembled through
  By night's departing grief.
Come to me, sunlight, come!
  Kiss me and make me fair,
Warm me and bear me home
  Into the realms of air!

Breeze of the summer, rise!
  Lift but the quivering spray,
Then I shall see the skies
  Beckon me far away.
I am a fragile thing
  Born of the sun and sea:
The touch of an insect's wing
  Is the rush of storm to me.

Mirroring tree and sky,
  A world within me lies,
And lights in my depths may vie
  With glances of beauty's eyes.
I shall be lost to sight,
  Won by the warm, sweet day;
My leaf, at the fall of night,
  Shall bear but a dust of gray.

LATE IN NOVEMBER.

The last sweet leaf—a golden leaf,
   Still touched with emerald, flushed with red,—
Hangs fluttering in its happy grief,
   A souvenir of summer dead.
The winds have blown, the woods are strown
   With spoils from all the fading year;
But who shall moan when seeds are sown
   Whence bud and bloom shall reappear?

Down many a smiling water-way
   The willows swish in lithe delight
Their tawny tentacles that sway
   In rhythmic motion day and night.
With nut-browned hands November stands
   And vacillates 'twixt cloud and sun.
O'er bottom lands the fog expands
   Its smoky shroud when day is done.

Old winter hovers in the mist
   Of gray that blurs the wooded hill,
Where hardy camphor flowers resist
   His skirmish line with hero will.
Brown fields of corn that moan forlorn
   And flaunt their tatters on the wind,
All stripped and torn in hasty scorn,
   Stand empty like the dotard's mind.

And so the year wanes to its close;
   And so the winter draweth nigh,
When earth shall take her brief repose,
   And sleep and rest when storms are high.
When winds are loud and, like a shroud,
   The snow lies white on hill and vale,
Then dreams shall crowd where age sits bowed,
   Repeating youth's remembered tale.

But in sheathed buds are baby leaves,
   Close curled in seeds are flower and tree,
And when spring's martins seek the eaves
   And from his hive escapes the bee,
Then all day long shall bloom and song
   Proclaim life's victories full and sweet,
And lovers throng and hope be strong
   And children run on eager feet.

For nature never balks nor fails,
   Nor makes one season spoil the rest;
Her promise buds when spring prevails,
   Grows strong when summer fareth best;
Matures complete and full and sweet
   When autumn ripens into peace;
Then snow and sleet and storm repeat
   Their yearly toil for life's increase.

Late in November, yet a hint
   Of summer joy makes glad the sky;
And still perfumes of flower and mint
   On vagrant breezes wander by,

So man grows old, the warm blood cold,
  And yet the soul is still aware
Of manifold delights untold
  And love's compulsion in the air.

Is still aware that heaven bends low
  To warm the earth and paint the sky;
And hope displays the promised bow
  On clouds of doubt that wander by:
Is still aware of that sweet care
  That notes the sparrows as they fall
And through despair or trust doth bear,
  Or soon or late, some good for all.

*CASCO BAY

If e'er you sail on Casco Bay
    When fields are green and skies are sweet,
And watch the foam-capped waves at play
    Where land and sea touch hands and greet,
As friend with friend, in rude delight;
    Your soul, like birds at break of day,
Will rise for many a joyous flight
    Midst summer isles of Casco Bay:
        Of Casco Bay! Sweet Casco Bay!
        Where life is joy and love at play
        Midst summer isles of Casco Bay.

Oh, wild and glad and circling far,
    The ripples sparkle from your prow
As silvery laughter from a star
    When Venus decks the evening's brow;
And where the islands stand apart,
    The ocean waves roll in to pay
Some tribute from the sea's great heart
    To gentle, queenly Casco Bay:
        To Casco Bay! Dear Casco Bay!
        Your soul imbibes the salt-sea spray,
        And sings with lovely Casco Bay.

° My thanks are due to the Century Company for permission to use Casco Bay in this volume.

Down smiling channels shadows run
   And shimmer on the green blue tides;
And, booming like a far-off gun,
   Where Harpswell sea from sea divides,
You hear the breakers' sullen roar
   And watch the waves ascend in spray,
While all around, behind, before,
   The white sails swell on Casco Bay:
     On Casco Bay! Fair Casco Bay!
     The white sails fill and bear away
     The happy ships on Casco Bay.

LIGHTER MEASURES.

THE TIDE MILL.

The tide flows in and the tide flows out,
    And the miller stands at his seaward door,
And the sailors hail him with song and shout
    While the mill grinds on and the breakers roar.

They have harnessed the wave to the creaking wheel,
    And it sighs at its toil in a lonesome way,
And barnacles crust on the slimy keel
    Of the slow barge loitering down the bay.

But the barge is rich with the tide mill's gain,
    And the miller smiles as the sunlight streams
Athwart its sails, and forgets the pain
    Of his daily task in its golden gleams.

Sail on, O bark! to the hungry town,
    With the snowy wealth of the old tide mill,
As the stones go round and the tide runs down,
    And the white dust settles on roof and sill.

Sail on, O, barge! there are mouths to fill
    In the skipper's cot on the lobster boat;
And the shining coins for the miller's till
    May gather rust as you idly float.

The miller he winketh his leeward eye,
    For a thrifty miller and wise is he,
And he sings, as the mackerel smacks go by,
    A lusty song of the fog-bound sea.

But all the while that he vows to wait
  For the "white, white ship with the white, white
      sail,"
He thinks of a cot and a wicker gate,
  And a baby lass, and her mother pale,

Still sewing there in the porch's shade;
  And he thanks his stars for the salt sea tide,
That ebbs for the mother and flows for the maid,
  And grinds for the matron as once for the bride.

And he shouts his joy to the laughing sea,
  And the skippers laugh back as they sail away,
For a merry miller and wise is he
  As his barge goes loitering down the bay.

THE MORTGAGE.

I dont mind the wind and the weather,
  The blizzard, the thaw or the freeze,
But when the crops fail, then we gather
  The mortgage's surplus of squeeze.

Perhaps if we had a full season
  Of seed-time and harvest and fruit,
And prices were good, there'd be reason
  To put forth a resolute foot.

But, somehow, I feel, to my sorrow,
  A small scrap of paper outweighs
All wisdom and strength I can borrow,
  Or force from the strength of my days.

I must sleep, I grow old, I grow weary,
  The mortgage eats on night and day;
When the winter is songless and dreary,
  It is sucking my life-blood away,

And delights in my misery, and makes me
  A fool to the gay or the wise;
And if I would flee it o'ertakes me,
  Reproach in its hunger-grown eyes.

Like the star fish that feeds on the oyster,
  Like the soulless old man of the sea,
It clings, this insatiate roysterer,
  This glutinous glutton, to me.

"You wrong me, you grieve me, you make me
  Seem hard and unfeeling and bad,"
The slimy thing whispers. "Forsake me!"
  I cry, "you are driving me mad!"

It only clings closer and closer,
  And mocks at my pitiful need;
When we both breathe our last, the disposer
  Will resurrect it as a deed;

But I shall go naked and bleeding
  Where thousands of mortgagors throng,
In the limbo of souls where all pleading
  And innocent creatures belong.

And should I go thence up to heaven,
  Or hades, or — well, anywhere,
I'll rejoice in whatever is given,
  Provided no mortgage is there.

THE FIRST CAWS.

He sits aloft on the ragged fir,
  A blotch of midnight above the snow,
With his shining, impatient wings astir,
  While peering and nodding and bowing low,
As if to awaken some quick applause
For the first of his spring-announcing caws.

Look out for your fresh eggs, speckled hen!
  Have a care for your darlings, goosey gray!
So sure as the spring time comes again
  He'll bring his harem and court this way,
And eggs and goslings, by natural laws,
Are treasure trove to this prince of caws.

He may shiver and shake in the biting cold,
  But he knows that the sun is climbing high,
And the heart within him is true and bold,
  Though his methods are thought to be
          somewhat sly;
So he pluckily waits till the ice drift thaws,
Then hails the spring with a song of caws.

A hardy old pioneer is he
  Who forces his way to the frozen north,
And the months that follow will surely see —
  A tribute of praise to his valorous worth —
Long lines of followers, black as haws,
Joining their own with his moving caws.

TO JOHN CLARK RIDPATH.

On completing his fiftieth year. (Written for the celebration of that event, April 27, 1891.)

I once heard a story related, or sung,
Of a jolly old chap who forever was young;
Who wasted no time in bemoaning his fate.
When spring greens were backward and robins were
      late,
When frosts nipped the beans and the hens ceased to
      lay,
And it rained every night and blew cold every day;
While the newspapers grumbled about the hard times,
And the augur-eyed critic dissected his rhymes,
His smile put on features more broadly sublime;
And "'twill all come out right in the best of good
      time!"
Was the saying he doted upon, I've been told,
Even after he grew to be fifty years old.

And, man, I remember as clear as can be,
When I was a boy in eighteen eighty-three,
And they came and cried out in my tender young ears
"Today you will finish your first fifty years!"
How I thought of the things that my grandfather told
Of the way a man feels when he gets to be old;
And I felt of myself, body, spirit and brain,
And wondered why people at fifty complain
That old age is coming with frowns on his face,
When they're just fairly started in life's earnest race.

At fifty, my lad, we begin to suspect
That we don't know it all, that we are not elect,
Among men, to bear all of the burdens of all,
From th' latest ward caucus to man's primal fall;
And hence if one have a whole heart and a mind
That to knowledge and sweetness and truth is
      inclined,
The half-century mark may not bode him great ill,
Nor the sun in its path be invoked to stand still
Till he overthrow Ammon, in slaughter and tears,
That his valor may win some proud mark for his
      years.

He has won his own kingdom, his soul and himself,
And when death shall lay him at last on the shelf,
As a volume that served its small day and was food
For minds that were groping their way to the good,
He shall go with the calmest assurance and trust
That worth shall not always be prisoned in dust;
For worth is still worth, be it humble or great,
And love ever holds the divinest estate.

As we learn of man's cruelty, hatred and sin,
We are taught in what frailties his errors begin;
And the soul that is wise will but deepen in love,
As from childhood and innocence forward we move;
And he groweth old with the tenderest grace
Who keepeth still warm in his spirit's embrace
That perennial youth which, like mercy, remains
A support to the soul, as the wealth of sweet rains
Is food to the lily and strength to the oak,

Till life yields to frost or the lumberman's stroke.
So all is summed up in the words that were said
By the instrument-maker, whose long look ahead
Was fraught with philosophy, full of the wise
And homely good sense that links man to the skies—
"Keep a conscience that's void of offense in God's
          sight,
And keep all the nautical instruments bright!"

SOCIETY VERSE.

O, give me a poem with blood in its veins,
  A soul in its pulse, and a flow
That swells like the rush of a stream after rains
  When the mountains are losing their snow.

Or give me a song that comes warm from the heart,
  With a pathos that melts into tears,
Or a melody wrought from the echoes that start
  From the tomb of the long-buried years:

And I can go out on "a fine poet rave,"
  And dream with your dreamer all night;
And sing every star to its luminous grave
  In the blush of the morning's delight.

But when you come in with your lavender rhymes,
  Your sapless and motionless things;
Your rose-tinted saw-dust and ice-tinkered chimes
  And fancies with gold foil for wings;

Then pray let me sleep the sweet sleep of the just,
  Like all things that nature esteems;
And when the birds wake me, as one from the dust,
  You will not have troubled my dreams.

SERVICE.

To serve the wise, or good, or great,
Were surely no ill-ordered fate;
E'en grievous toil might well be borne,
And soul and body, service worn,
Might feel the joy of having wrought
For princely worth or kingly thought.

But service forced from you, but once,
By some conceited, place proud dunce,
Some empty prig who thinks it meet
To tread your manhood 'neath his feet,
Becomes an evil to your thought,
A mountain sorrow shaped and wrought
By hands ignoble, a growing shame
Whose burden leaves you bent and lame
And hurt in spirit; a disgrace
That meets you often face to face,
And laughs and chuckles at your plight,
And in fine scorn says "Served you right!
You cringed to him of little worth,
And let him crush you to the earth;
Now bow to me through all the years
And pay the tribute of your tears,
And walk with me your little span
For having thus been less than man."

TO OUR SINGING DOCTOR.

J. N. M.

Dear Galen, I thank thee again for thy singing,
As one thanks the robins that herald the spring,
    When brows that are aching
    And hearts that are breaking
Are mended because of the promise they bring.

Through woods, over meadows my love fareth
    winging,
For, "bard of the prairies," my soul clings to thee
    As mists to the fountain,
    As clouds to the mountain,
As islanders cling to their crofts by the sea.

No pink teas inspire thee with frigid emotion
To twitter in triolets over ice cream;
    Nor yet may those measures
    That scorn the rich treasures
Of music and melody utter thy dream.

The voice of the prairies, the breath of devotion,
Up fresh from the sod, from the blossom, the tree,
    In summer exhaling
    Are still the prevailing
Provokers of song to the spirit of thee.

Like ancient Anacreon, to love and love's longing
Thou touchest a harp with no note out of tune;
  The snows may be flying,
  Eurocklydon crying,
But when thou art singing 'tis always sweet June.

O, bard of the prairies! long may thy dreams
  thronging
Flow into men's souls with their raptures divine;
  May glad intimations
  And rare divinations
And forecasts of paradise ever be thine.

TWO SIDES OF A QUESTION.

An owl that dozed in a hollow tree,
  Heard a sparrow's ground notes ringing;
"A fig for such chirruppy stuff," said he!
"I grant there's enough as to quantity,
But alack and alas! as to quality,
  By my soul it is not singing."

"O, beautiful owl, O, sunbright owl!
  Up there in thy fair dominions,"
The sparrows twittered, "come down sweet fowl,
And learn that a sparrow is not an owl
  To share thy broad opinions.

"For the sparrow he chirpeth soft and low
  Where the brooklet runs with laughter,
And the sun shines fair and the daisies grow;
But the owl he waits till the night hangs low,
  And then comes hooting after."

AFTERNOON PHILOSOPHY.

I have written some reason, some rhyme,
Have tried to be solemn, sublime;
Have bored for the fountain of tears
And only reached gas, as the years
Have drifted and faded away,
Like the songs and the sighs of a day.

But now, when a new year comes in, —
It may be a sorrow, a sin,
A thing that foreshadows decay, —
I trifle and pause and delay,
And turn back to June and the rose,
And hug the grate close when it snows,
And murmur and mutter and scold
At the manners, the times and the cold.

Such cold, too! not hearty and strong,
Like the old winter days with their throng
Of labors, delights and good cheer,
That welcomed the birth of the year;
But, creeping, and sneaking, and damp,
It assails you with shiver and cramp,
And goes to your marrow and brings
A thousand rheumatical stings.

I'm not getting old; on my word,
Such a thought is extremely absurd;
It's the fashions, the people, the times;

Society, fiction and rhymes
That are all out of joint, and you know
Our snow's not at all like the snow
That fell when the country was new
And the linsey-clad lassies were true.

But ho, and heigh ho! here the boys
And the girls, with their chatter and noise,
Come rolicking in from the street
With wind-painted cheeks and glad feet;
And my eye feels the blur of a tear,
For I vow it's the same old new year
That we welcomed two score years ago
With the bells and the shouts and the flow
Of laughter and song, and the lone
Shrill cry of the late lover's tone,
"I'm here with my sleigh, Maud, alone!"

Youth only is youth, I'm aware,
But wrinkles and doubt and gray hair,
And the sorrow of life and the core
Of all sorrows that mortals deplore
For the sweet might-have-been folly slew
When the long days of morning were new,
Are forgotten and quite blotted out
When the children with laughter and shout
Come in at love's wide-open door
And bring us the morning once more.

You may theorize all that you may,
You may give your philosophy sway,
Or with maxim and dogma engage

To check the advances of age,
Yet I say and repeat and repeat,
That the shuttle of juvenile feet,
And the gladness of juvenile joy,
Bubbling up from the heart of a boy,
Or the soul of a girl, as the flow
Of sunshine that warms with its glow,
Can bring back the spirit of youth,
The light of its innocent truth,
A thousand times over again,
Where all wisdom of speech or of pen
Would fail in life's age-folded wing
To incite one soft flutter of spring.

You may sing what the young owe the old,
And it is as a tale that is told;
But yield the sweet gift to my tongue
To sing what the old owe the young,
And I will reply with a song
That shall bring back the days that were long,
That shall wake 'neath the mid-winter moon
The love-lighted evenings of June,
And the longing of youth and the tears,
And the multiplied bliss of the years.

AU REVOIR.

One sings alone for joy of song,
  And one for hope of gain;
Another sings for dreams that throng
  The paths of doubt and pain.

And who shall win and who shall wait,
  Whose songs the people heed?
When nights are old and moons are late,
  Whose lonely heart shall bleed?

For hearts must bleed and men must wait,
  And many a bard must fail,
And some sit cold and desolate
  When snows of age prevail.

I, who have never dared to claim
  The poet's right divine,
Have wrought in love's benignant name
  These faltering lays of mine.

They gushed from out an ardent soul
  That nature bade to sing,
And if they fail of art's control,
  Or want the flow and swing

That give the lyric muse her power,
  I shall not bow in shame,
But pray for some immortal dower
  Of love's diviner flame.

And toiling down the western slope
　Where evening shadows throng,
I fain would garner sweeter hope
　In richer sheaves of song.

But if this may not be, O, friends!
　And I should strive in vain,
And walk unknown where day-light ends
　And nights are dark with rain;

Pray speak but this for my poor art;
　"He missed the call divine,
But never stooped to wound a heart
　Or print a cruel line."

www.ingramcontent.com/pod-product-compliance
Lightning Source LLC
Chambersburg PA
CBHW032146010726
47493CB00008BA/2601